For Safta
—G.S.

For Adam, thank you for making my life
a little bit sweeter and my days a little sunnier.
—L.C.

Dial Books for Young Readers
An imprint of Penguin Random House LLC, New York

First published in the United States of America by Dial Books for Young Readers,
an imprint of Penguin Random House LLC, 2021

Visit us online at penguinrandomhouse.com.

Library of Congress Cataloging-in-Publication Data is available.

Manufactured in China
ISBN 9780735228283

1 3 5 7 9 10 8 6 4 2

Design by Mina Chung • Text set in Edmondsans

IT BEGAN WITH LEMONADE

by GIDEON STERER   illustrated by LIAN CHO

dial books for young readers

It was the first Saturday of summer,
hot as an oven with blazing blue skies,
and I hoped to sell some lemonade.

I chopped and measured, squeezed and stirred, tinkered, tweaked

and tasted, until I had something delicious.

Then, carefully, I loaded my wagon and rolled outside to find . . .

there was no room for me.

Not on my street.

Not on
Bobby Tillman's
street.

Not on my
grandma Rose's
street.

Nowhere.

the pavement
sizzled.

The sun scorched,

So I kept walking.

And just as I was about to give up,

all my bad luck . . .

got worse.

If you've never chased a runaway
lemonade stand out of town,

through the woods,

and

across

a meadow,

it's no fun.

So when at last I reached the river,

I was ready to cry.

I sat for a long while,
feeling terrible as a turnip,

when, from around the bend . . .

came something thirsty.

I straightened up, and hung my sign.

I said.

The old man tipped his hat.

"Lemonade,

I called out to the water.

And again,

lemonade!"

from around the bend

"COOL" LEMONADE

came something thirsty.

Soon came things with **paws,**

and **claws**,

and as I looked out from that riverbank,
it felt just like a dream.

"COOL"
MONADE

25¢

TIPS

One after another they floated by,
each thirstier than the last,

larger, stranger,

sippers, slurpers,

and I tried my best to keep up. But the river was still thirsty.

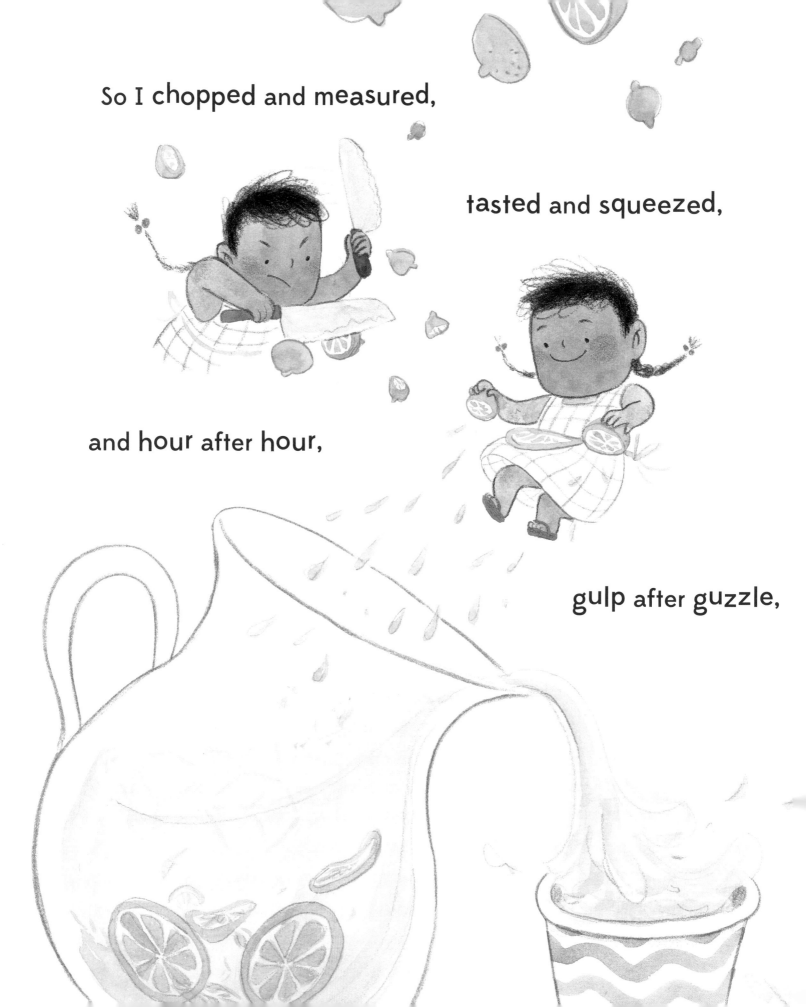

So I chopped and measured,

tasted and squeezed,

and hour after hour,

gulp after guzzle,

this is what I called:

Lemonade!
Lemonade!
A glass for you,
half price for two!

Beat the heat, frosty sweet! Swim on over... Swim right up!

For you, and you, for all!

Get it now while it lasts...

It took some time to fill those glasses,

but fill them I did,

and out beneath the sinking sun . . .

we drank
our lemonade.

The whole way home I smiled, thinking of tomorrow.

And late that night, deep asleep,
I saw what it could be.